D.I.Y. MAKE IT HAPPEN

DOCUMENTARY FILM

VIRGINIA LOH-HAGAN

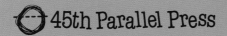
45th Parallel Press

Published in the United States of America by Cherry Lake Publishing
Ann Arbor, Michigan
www.cherrylakepublishing.com

Reading Adviser: Marla Conn MS, Ed., Literacy specialist, Read-Ability, Inc.
Book Designer: Felicia Macheske

Photo Credits: © PHILIPIMAGE/Shutterstock.com, cover, 1; © Jeffrey M Horler/Shutterstock.com, 3; © tinka's/Shutterstock.com, 5; © Kues/Shutterstock.com, 7; © Michaelpuche/Shutterstock.com, 9; © photka/Shutterstock.com, 10;© timquo/Shutterstock.com, 10; © Monkey Business Images/Shutterstock.com, 11; © Chanwit Ohm/Shutterstock.com, 12; © Ruslan Rizvanov/Shutterstock.com, 14; © c12/Shutterstock.com, 14;© goodluz/Shutterstock.com, 15; © Africa Studio/Shutterstock.com, 17; © tobkatrina/Shutterstock.com, 18, 30; © goir/Shutterstock.com, 19, 31; © Iakov Filimonov/Shutterstock.com, 20; © Elnur/Shutterstock.com, 21; © atthaphong Ekariyasap/Shutterstock.com, 22; © PHILIPIMAGE/Shutterstock.com, 23, 25; © gualtiero boffi/Shutterstock.com, 27; © Syda Productions/Shutterstock.com, 29; © imagedb.com/Shutterstock.com, 31; © wavebreakmedia/Shutterstock.com, back cover; © Dora Zett/Shutterstock.com, back cover

Graphic Elements Throughout: © pashabo/Shutterstock.com; © axako/Shutterstock.com; © IreneArt/Shutterstock.com; © Katya Bogina/Shutterstock.com; © Belausava Volha/Shutterstock.com; © Nik Merkulov/Shutterstock.com; © Ya Tshey/Shutterstock.com; © kubais/Shutterstock.com; © Sasha Nazim/Shutterstock.com; © Infomages/Shutterstock.com; © Ursa Major/Shutterstock.com; © topform/Shutterstock.com; © Art'nLera/Shutterstock.com; © graphics/Shutterstock.com; © primiaou/Shutterstock.com

45th Parallel Press is an imprint of Cherry Lake Publishing.

Library of Congress Cataloging-in-Publication Data has been filed and is available at catalog.loc.gov

Cherry Lake Publishing would like to acknowledge the work of The Partnership for 21st Century Skills.
Please visit *www.p21.org* for more information.

Printed in the United States of America
Corporate Graphics

ABOUT THE AUTHOR

Dr. Virginia Loh-Hagan is an author, university professor, former classroom teacher, and curriculum designer. She likes watching documentary films. She lives in San Diego with her very tall husband and very naughty dogs. To learn more about her, visit www.virginialoh.com.

TABLE OF CONTENTS

CHAPTER ONE

WHAT DOES IT MEAN TO MAKE A DOCUMENTARY FILM?

Do you love filming? Do you love true stories? Do you love researching? Do you love talking to people? Then, making a **documentary** film is the right project for you!

Documentary films are nonfiction movies. Nonfiction means true. These films document history. They document reality. **Document** means to record. It's proof that something happened.

Documentaries are about real events. They're about real people. They're about past events. They're about current events. They can be funny. They can be sad. They can be silly. They can be shocking.

Watch documentary films.

KNOW THE LINGO

Aerial shot: a shot from high above

Archival footage: video clips from past films

Boom: a long pole used to hold cameras or microphones

Clip: a brief segment cut from a film

Close-up: a movie shot that fills up the screen

Cut: when one scene ends and a new scene starts

Dissolve: when scenes blend together

Montage: a mix of shots that are put together

Pan: a shot that moves from left to right taken from a camera that stays in the same spot

Soft focus: blurry effect

Take: unedited footage

Tracking shot: shot using a moving camera

Two shot: shot of two people from the waist up

They're shown on TV. They're shown in movie theaters. They're shown on the Internet. They can be long. They can be short.

Filmmakers make movies. Documentary filmmakers stick to the truth. They can't make up things. But they still create stories. They create a point of view. They create a message. They create questions. They ask questions. They answer questions. They share facts with viewers. Viewers watch movies. They watch shows.

You'll have fun! You'll meet lots of people. You'll research. The best part is learning more about your topic.

Learn from other filmmakers.

PROD. NO.
SCENE | TAKE | ROLL
TE | | SOUND
OD. CO.
RECTOR
AMERAMAN

CHAPTER TWO

WHAT DO YOU NEED TO MAKE A DOCUMENTARY FILM?

Learn how films are made.

➡ Take classes. Take lessons.

➡ Work on a movie set. Do this for free. Get experience.

Raise money. It costs money to make films.

➡ Host events. Charge people.

➡ Ask people to give money.

➡ Get a job. Save your money.

➡ Don't accept money from subjects. Subjects are the people in your movie.

Make a budget. Budgets track money.

➡ **Track money earned.**

➡ **Track money spent.**

➡ **Don't spend more than you have.**

➡ **Find ways to save money.**

Take online classes about filmmaking.

Get equipment to make videos. You have several choices. Use what you can pay for. Use what's easy for you.

⇒ **Use a smartphone. Smartphones have cameras. This is the most mobile option. Mobile means easy to move. Smartphones can go anywhere.**

⇒ **Use a webcam. A webcam is a camera. It's on a computer. It's above the monitor.**

⇒ **Use a video recording device. An example is a camcorder. Transfer videos to computers.**

⇒ **Use microphones. Microphones improve the sound. Make sure voices are clear. Make sure voices are loud. Make sure viewers can hear everything.**

Look for used equipment. Save money.

Get online tools. This lets you fix videos.

➡ **Use or borrow a computer. Make sure it has lots of storage space. Storage holds data. It's the computer's memory. Videos need a lot of storage.**

➡ **Use the Internet.**

➡ **Get video editing tools. Some are free online. Some cost money.**

Focus on a topic. Topics are what the films are about.

➡ **Love your topic.**

➡ **Share ideas with others. Ask what they think. You need a topic that people care about.**

➡ **Find an interesting angle. Shed new light on the topic.**

➡ **Focus on fun facts. Think of things most people don't know.**

➡ **Consider current issues. Challenge people's thinking.**

Give your film a purpose.

TRY THIS!

Create a promotion campaign. Spark people's interest. Share fun facts about your film. Create very short videos. These videos are commercials. Feature facts from A to Z.

You'll need: YouTube, social media, computer, Internet, videos

Steps

1 Research your film topic. Find interesting facts. List them from A to Z. Don't use facts you're presenting in the film.

2 Create 26 videos. Make them 30 seconds long. Each video should focus on a specific letter.

3 Upload them to YouTube.

4 Release a video a day. Do this a month before your first film screening.

5 Post fun facts on social media. Do this the same day as the video.

Choose the type of film you want to make.
There are different types.

→ **Expository** films present the truth. They include all sides of the issue.

→ **Observational** films are like reality shows. They film what happens. They film as things happen.

→ **Interactive** films include subjects. They include you interviewing subjects.

→ **Reflexive** films are when people talk to the camera.

→ Some films have a "voice of God" **narrator**. Narrators comment. They tell viewers what's going on. They tell viewers what to think.

→ Some films combine different types.

Get a crew. Crew members are helpers.

➡ **Get people to work cameras.**

➡ **Get people to help with lighting.**

Work with people who like your topic.

CHAPTER THREE

HOW DO YOU MAKE A DOCUMENTARY FILM?

Do a lot of research. Learn about your topic.

→ Read **primary sources**. Read firsthand accounts. This includes letters. This includes interviews.

→ Read **secondary sources**. These are by experts. Experts study the topic.

→ Watch films about your topic.

→ Read online articles.

→ Talk to people. Get their stories.

Use your research.

➡ **Narrow your topic.**

➡ **Find sources. Include them in the film.**

Name your film. A good title is key.

➡ **Connect it to the topic.**

➡ **Make it catchy. You want viewers to remember it.**

➡ **Be different from other films. Be unique.**

Check to see if your title is already taken.

ZURIEL ODUWOLE

Zuriel Oduwole lives in California. Her parents are from Africa. She is one of "the world's youngest filmmakers." She started at age 9. She entered school contests. By age 12, she had made four documentaries. She focuses on African issues. She filmed about the Ghana revolution. She filmed about being poor. She filmed about girls' education. She interviewed presidents. She interviewed business leaders. She taught herself. She uses online editing tools. She uses online voice tools. She said, "As I edit, produce, set up, and write the scripts for my documentaries, I have to learn a lot of things." Oduwole advises doing a lot of research. She advises learning more about filmmaking.

SCENE   TAKE

Day Night Interior Exterior Mos
Filter   Sync

Get parents' permission to film anyone under age 18.

Describe your film.

⇒ Let viewers know what your film is about.

⇒ Make it fun.

⇒ Keep it brief.

Know the laws.

⇒ Be fair. Don't take sides.

⇒ Avoid **conflicts of interest**. Don't have connections with your subjects.

⇒ Present people in a fair way. Present your topic in a fair way.

⇒ Respect copyright laws. People own their work. Get their permission. Or, pay to use their work. Create your own content. Use content the public can use.

⇒ Get people to sign consent forms. Consent means permission. Get people's permission to be in your film. Get permission to use places.

Make viewers believe in your issue.

Interview people. Include these interviews in your film. Include the parts that make sense.

→ **Choose experts. Choose people who know your topic.**

→ **Write questions before meeting. Be prepared.**

→ **Ask questions. Keep a conversational style. Get people to talk to you. Don't make it too formal.**

→ **Film people's responses. Collect footage. Footage is anything filmed. Film everything. Cut footage later.**

Write a script. Scripts are outlines.

→ **Plan how long your film will be. Plan every minute.**

→ **Write out each scene. Write out talking parts. Know what you want to film.**

→ **Plan ahead. Plan schedules. This will save time.**

→ **Film the scenes you need.**

Start filming.

➡ **Act out scenes. Use the true stories. Get actors.**

➡ **Consider including an epilogue. This is a closing comment.**

➡ **Find a setting. Know where you want to film.**

➡ **Get live footage. Film events as they happen. Collect sounds.**

➡ **Film establishing shots. These shots create the mood.**

➡ **Film B-roll. This is footage of objects. It's footage of locations. It's the background.**

Remember that sometimes less is more.

Edit your film.

➡ **Delete scenes. Stay on topic.**

➡ **Cut different scenes. Put them together. Create a story.**

➡ **Create a score. Scores are music. Add music to your film.**

➡ **Include pictures. Include interviews. Include footage.**

➡ **Create voice-overs. Narrate scenes. Talk over scenes.**

➡ **Combine film and sound.**

CHAPTER FOUR

HOW DO YOU PROMOTE A DOCUMENTARY FILM?

You've got a film. Now, you need to get viewers!

Create hype. Hype is excitement.

➡ Create a trailer. Trailers are like commercials. They're short videos about the film. They attract viewers.

➡ Make trailers exciting. Grab viewers' attention.

➡ Show bits of your film. These are called teasers.

Promote the film.

➡ **Use social media. Create a Web site. Create a Facebook page. Post on Twitter.**

➡ **Tell everyone you know.**

➡ **Tell people to spread the word.**

➡ **Make flyers. Flyers are information on a page. Hang them up. Send to people.**

Be excited about your film.

QUICK TIPS

- Make a film others want to see. Don't teach a lesson. Share a story.

- Don't make people sad. Make people mad. Anger is active. It inspires people.

- Focus on new ideas. Learn along with your viewers. Don't be a know-it-all.

- Use humor. Be funny. Be entertaining.

- Talk to people who disagree with you. Learn the other side of the story.

- Give copies of the film away. Give it away for free. This helps get the word out.

- Think about your next project. Use the buzz from your current project. Consider building on the same topic. Become an expert.

- Keep a diary. Write down what happens every day. Include mistakes. Include what went well.

Host a **screening**. Screenings are movie showings. Host a party.

⇨ Choose a night.

⇨ Choose a place. Consider a big house. Consider a room at school.

⇨ Invite people. Invite people who can review your film. Invite people who can promote your film. Invite your family. Invite your friends.

⇨ Give out snacks. An example is popcorn. Give out drinks.

⇨ Get dressed up.

⇨ Greet people as they come in.

⇨ Give a speech. Do this before the film starts. Introduce the film. Share your reason for making the film.

⇨ Thank everyone who helped. Thank everyone for coming. Let viewers ask you questions. Do this after you show the film.

Roll out the red carpet!

Submit your film to festivals. Film festivals review films. They select the best films. They give awards to films. Top winners get shown.

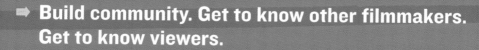 Look for festivals nearby. Most festivals are in large cities.

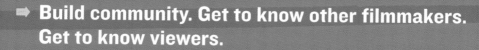 Pay the fees. Send in your film.

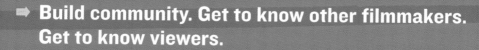 Hope your film gets chosen. Companies buy good films. They spend money to promote those films.

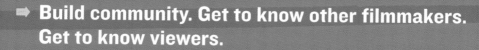 Get promoted. Festivals host events. They host panels. They host interviews.

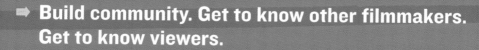 Build community. Get to know other filmmakers. Get to know viewers.

Ask people to write reviews. Good reviews help promote films.

➡ **Ask people what they liked.**

➡ **Ask people what they didn't like.**

➡ **Consider editing your film.**

Be tough. Listen to what people say.

D.I.Y. EXAMPLE!

STEPS	EXAMPLES
Topic	People and dogs
Title	"Are We Dog-Sweater People Now?"
Length	30 minutes
Description	What brings strangers together? Dogs! Every morning, our local park gets invaded. It's a dog invasion. Owners walk their dogs. People bring treats. They stop to talk. Buddy is the most popular dog. He dresses up in costumes. Everyone loves Buddy. Strangers become buddies because of Buddy. This documentary explores the community Buddy built.
Type	This film is a combination. It's interactive. I interview others. It's observational. I film Buddy for a day. It has "voice of God" narration. I talk about the film events. I talk over the footage.

STEPS	EXAMPLES
Script	Introduce the film.

Introduce the film.

 ⬥ Play slow piano music. Show title and credits.

 ⬥ Show B-roll of owners walking dogs.

Film first scene.

 ⬥ Include interviews of dog walkers.

 ⬥ Show pictures of people petting dogs.

Film second scene.

 ⬥ Show interviews with Buddy's owners and friends.

Film third scene.

 ⬥ Show footage of Buddy walking around the park. Narrate.

Film fourth scene.

 ⬥ Show B-roll of people talking to each other.

 ⬥ Include epilogue. Give commentary. Talk about how dogs make us more human. Dog costumes make people laugh. They bring people together.

GLOSSARY

conflicts of interest (KAHN-flikts UHV IN-trist) not having any connections or relationships with the subjects; being fair

document (DAHK-yuh-muhnt) to record

documentary (dahk-yuh-MEN-tur-ee) nonfiction film

epilogue (EP-uh-lawg) ending commentary

establishing shots (ih-STAB-lish-ing SHAHTS) film shots that create the mood or set the scene

expository (ik-SPAH-zih-tor-ee) intended to explain or inform

footage (FUT-ij) everything filmed

hype (HIPE) excitement

interactive (in-tur-AK-tiv) when filmmakers talk to subjects

mobile (MOH-buhl) easy to move

narrator (NAR-ay-tur) the person telling the story

observational (ahb-zur-VAY-shuh-nuhl) filming events as they happen when they happen

primary sources (PRYE-mair-ee SORS-iz) firsthand accounts like letters and interviews

reflexive (rih-FLEKS-iv) when people talk to the camera

screening (SKREEN-ing) movie or film showing

script (SKRIPT) outline or guideline

secondary sources (SEK-uhn-der-ee SORS-iz) secondhand accounts in which experts write about the topic

teasers (TEEZ-urz) bits of a film shown to get people interested

trailer (TRAY-lur) video that previews a film

INDEX

LEARN MORE

BOOKS

Artis, Anthony Q. *The Shut Up and Shoot Documentary Guide: A Down & Dirty DV Production*. New York: Focal Press, 2014.

Ciampa, Rob, Theresa Moore, and John Caruccci. *YouTube Channels for Dummies*. Hoboken, NJ: Wiley & Sons, 2015.

Cornwall, Phyllis. *Online Etiquette and Safety*. Ann Arbor, MI: Cherry Lake Publishing, 2010.

Hewitt, John, and Gustavo Vazquez. *Documentary Filmmaking: A Contemporary Field Guide*. New York: Oxford University Press, 2013.

WEB SITES

The Alliance for Media Arts and Culture: www.thealliance.media

Creative Commons: www.creativecommons.org

International Documentary Association: www.documentary.org

PBS—Youth Filmmaking Programs: www.pbs.org/pov/filmmakers/resources/youth-filmmaking-programs.php

WikiHow—How to Make a YouTube Video: www.wikihow.com/Make-a-YouTube-Video